KU-630-495

This Ladybird Book belongs to:

_____

_____

_____

_____

All children have a great ambition … to read by themselves.

Through traditional and popular stories, each title in the **Read It Yourself** series introduces children to the most commonly used words in the English language (*Key Words*), plus additional words necessary to tell the story.
The additional words appearing in this book are listed below.

hen, sly, fox,
dizzy, falls, sleep, asleep,
stones, splashes, gone

A catalogue record for this book is available
from the British Library

Published by Ladybird Books Ltd Loughborough Leicestershire UK
Ladybird Books Inc Auburn Maine 04210 USA

© LADYBIRD BOOKS LTD 1993

LADYBIRD and the device of a Ladybird are trademarks of Ladybird Books Ltd

All rights reserved. No part of this publication may be reproduced,
stored in a retrieval system, or transmitted in any form or by any
means, electronic, mechanical, photocopying, recording or otherwise,
without the prior consent of the copyright owner.

Sly Fox
and
Red Hen

by Fran Hunia

illustrated by John Dyke

Here is Red Hen.
Her home is in
a tree.

This is Sly Fox.

He wants to eat
Red Hen.

I will go and look
for Red Hen,
he says.

Sly Fox looks
for Red Hen.

He has a bag.

Red Hen is in her home
up in the tree.

Red Hen comes down for some water.

Sly Fox jumps up
into the tree.

Red Hen comes home.

Sly Fox is here,
says Red Hen.

I have to jump up.

Red Hen is up here.

She says,
You can't jump
up here, Sly Fox.
Go home.

Sly Fox says,
I can't go up to you,
Red Hen.
You will have
to come down here.

No, I will not,
says Red Hen.

Yes, you will,
says Sly Fox.

Sly Fox runs round and round.

Red Hen looks down at him.

Sly Fox runs
round and round.

Red Hen is dizzy.

Red Hen falls down,
down, down.

Sly Fox has the bag.
Red Hen falls
into it.

I will go home
and eat Red Hen,
says Sly Fox.
Home we go.

Sly Fox runs
and runs.

It is hot.

Sly Fox wants
to sleep.

Sly Fox is asleep.

Red Hen gets out
of the bag.

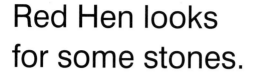

Red Hen looks
for some stones.

The stones go
into the bag.

I like this,
says Red Hen.

Red Hen runs home.

Sly Fox looks up.

He says,
Red Hen is in the bag.
I will go home
and eat her up.

Sly Fox runs home.

He says,
I will put Red Hen
into the hot water.

Red Hen is not
in the bag.

The stones are
in the bag.

They fall
into the water.

The hot water
splashes Sly Fox.

Red Hen likes
her home in the tree.

Sly Fox will not come
to look for her.
He has gone.

LADYBIRD
READING SCHEMES

Read It Yourself links with all Ladybird reading schemes and can be used with any other method of learning to read.

Say the Sounds

Ladybird's **Say the Sounds** graded reading scheme is a *phonics* scheme. It teaches children the sounds of individual letters and letter combinations, enabling them to tackle new words by building them up as a blend of smaller units.

There are 8 titles in this scheme:

1 **Rocket to the jungle**
2 **Frog and the lollipops**
3 **The go-cart race**
4 **Pirate's treasure**
5 **Humpty Dumpty and the robots**
6 **Flying saucer**
7 **Dinosaur rescue**
8 **The accident**

Support material available: Practice Books, Double Cassette pack, Flash Cards